THIS BOOK IS DEDICATED TO THE MEMORY OF
MY PARENTS AND TO MY SISTERS AND BROTHER
WHO LIVED WITH ME IN TIR NA N-OG

—M. H.

FOR NEASA

—P. J. L.

Library of Congress Cataloging-in-Publication Data
Heaney, Marie.
The names upon the harp, Irish myth and legend / by Marie Heaney;
illustrated by P.J. Lynch.   p.   cm.
Contents: Moytura—The children of Lir—The birth of Cuchulainn—
Bricriu's feast—Deirdre of the sorrows—Finn and the salmon of
knowledge—The enchanted deer—Oisin in the land of youth.

ISBN 0-590-68052-8
1. Tales—Ireland. [1. Folklore—Ireland.] I. Lynch, Patrick James, ill. II.
Title. PZ8.1.H3465Nam 2000 398.2'09417—dc21 98-042103 CIP
10 9 8 7 6 5 4 3 2 1   0/0 01 02 03 04
Printed in Singapore   46
First Edition, November 2000

TABLE OF CONTENTS

AUTHOR'S NOTE

*"...you and I leave
names upon the harp"*
CUCHULAINN TO CONOR,
FROM *ON BAILE'S STRAND*
BY W. B. YEATS

HE STORIES IN THIS BOOK have been known to the Irish for centuries. They are preserved in manuscripts hundreds of years old, but long before they were written down by scribes in early Irish monasteries, they had been told at feasts and gatherings by storytellers and bards, and were still told until recently.

Scholars have divided early Irish literature into three main cycles: the Mythological cycle, the Ulster cycle, and the Fenian cycle. In this book, I have given a brief introduction to each of these cycles and included tales from each. But I have chosen the stories not merely because they are old or representative, but because they have entertained and moved listeners and readers for generations, and still have the power to do so.

THE MYTHOLOGICAL CYCLE

The Tuatha De Danaan, the People of the Goddess Danu, were a divine race who possessed great magical powers and were learned and gifted, according to Irish legend. They came to Ireland to take over the country, and when they landed, they set fire to their boats so there would be no turning back. The smoke from the burning boats darkened the sun and filled the land for three days, and the Fir Bolgs, who lived there, thought the Tuatha De Danaan had arrived in a magic mist.

The Tuatha De Danaan defeated the Fir Bolgs and became rulers of Ireland, but another enemy, the demonic Fomorians, enslaved and tyrannized them until they too were defeated at the battle of Moytura.

After this victory, the Tuatha De Danaan ruled Ireland for many years, until they were defeated by another wave of invaders, the Milesians. Although they were banished by these newcomers, they did not leave Ireland. Instead, they went underground to live in the *sidhes*, mounds and earthworks that are scattered all over the country.

Above them, the human inhabitants of Ireland, descendants of the Milesians, lived and died, and were helped but sometimes hindered by the Tuatha De Danaan, who became known as the People of the Sidhe, the Faery, or the Little Folk. From time to time, these mysterious beings would enter the mortal world, on Halloween and May Day in particular, to mingle with humans and come and go in their affairs. But they always returned to their kingdom under the earth, that happy otherworld, the Land of Youth.

MOYTURA

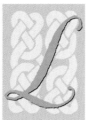ONG, LONG AGO IN IRELAND A GREAT BATTLE FOR MASTERY OF the island took place at Moytura. The struggle was between two powerful tribes: the Tuatha De Danaan and the Fomorians.

The Tuatha De Danaan were a divine people whose king, Nuada, ruled the country wisely and justly. At his court at Tara were feastings and entertainments of all kinds, and everyone had plenty to eat and drink.

Their enemies, the demonic Fomorians, were fierce sea-pirates who lived on the islands scattered round the western coast. Their leader was known as Balor of the Evil Eye and he was feared for his cruelty. It was through a magic spell that Balor had got his power and his name. One day when he was a boy he heard chanting inside the house where the magicians gathered to work new spells. Seeing a window open high in the wall, he scrambled up and looked furtively through it, but the room was so full of fumes and gases that he could see nothing. As he peered through the window the chants grew louder, and a strong plume of smoke rose in the air straight into Balor's face. Instantly he was blinded and could not open one of his eyes. He struggled to the ground, writhing with pain, and at that moment one of the magicians came out of the house. "That spell we were making was a spell of death," he said to Balor, "and the fumes from it have brought the power of death to your eye."

Among his own people Balor's eye remained shut, but when he opened it against his enemies, they dropped dead at his fearsome stare. As he grew older his eyelid grew heavier until, in the end, he could not open it without help. An ivory ring was driven though the lid and through this ring ropes were threaded to make a pulley. It took ten men to raise the great, heavy lid, but ten times that number were slain at a single glance. His evil eye made him of great importance to the Fomorians, and he became the most powerful of them all. His ships raided Ireland again and again, and Balor's pirates made slaves of the learned people of the Tuatha De Danaan.

But Balor had a secret fear. One of his druids had foretold that he would die at the hand of his own grandson. Balor had only one child, a daughter called Eithlinn, so he built a tower and shut the girl up in it with twelve women to guard her.

He warned the women that Eithlinn should never see a man, nor hear a man's name mentioned. With Eithlinn imprisoned in the tower Balor felt safe, for without a husband Eithlinn could not have a child and he could not die at his grandson's hand.

Eithlinn grew up into a beautiful woman, well cared for by her companions, but in spite of their kindness she felt lonely. The same man would appear to her again and again in her dreams, and she felt a longing to meet this person. And one day, through Balor's greed, she had her chance.

Balor had plenty of cattle, but he particularly coveted one wonderful cow, which belonged to Cian, a man of the Tuatha De Danaan. This marvelous cow never ran dry, and Balor wanted it so much that he would disguise himself and follow Cian around, waiting for a chance to seize the cow.

One day Balor saw Cian and his brother go to a forge to get some weapons made. Cian went into the forge while his brother stayed outside with the cow. Balor saw his chance. Turning himself into a redheaded boy, he went up to the man who stood with the cow and began to talk to him.

"Are you getting a sword made as well?" he asked.

"I am," said the brother, "in my turn. When Cian comes out of the forge he'll guard the cow and I'll go into the forge and get my weapon made."

"That's what you think!" said the boy. "Your brother has tricked you. He is using all the iron for himself, and there'll be none left for you!"

At this, the man stuffed the cow's halter into the boy's hand and ran into the forge to confront his brother. Instantly Balor threw off his disguise and dragged the cow back to the safety of his own island.

Cian was determined to retrieve his cow, so he went to a woman druid called Birog to ask for help.

Birog disguised Cian as a woman and then conjured up a wind so strong that she and Cian were carried off high in the air.

The wind dropped, and they landed safely on Balor's island at the foot of the tower where Eithlinn was imprisoned. Birog begged Eithlinn's guardians to let them in, saying they were escaping from enemies who wanted to kill them. The women took pity and agreed.

As soon as they were inside, Birog cast another spell and all the women, except Eithlinn, fell fast asleep. Cian, who had cast off his woman's clothes, ran up the stairs to the top of the tower. There, all alone, he found the most beautiful woman he had ever seen, gazing sadly out to sea. As he stared at her, Eithlinn turned round and recognized Cian as the one she had dreamt about so often. They were both overjoyed and, declaring their love for each other, they embraced with delight.

When morning came Cian wanted to take Eithlinn from her prison and bring her home with him, but Birog was so terrified of Balor that she swept Cian away from Eithlinn on another enchanted wind and took him back with her to Ireland. Eithlinn was brokenhearted when Cian left her, but she was comforted when she discovered that she would give birth to his child. In due course a boy was born, and she called him Lugh.

When Balor heard the news of his grandson's birth he made up his mind to kill the infant straight away and he gave orders that the baby be thrown into the sea. Wrapped in a blanket held in place by a pin, Lugh was cast into the current by Eithlinn's guardians. As the weeping women watched, the pin opened and the baby rolled into the sea, leaving the empty blanket spread over the waves. Balor felt safe once more. Now he had no grandson to bring about his end.

But Lugh had been saved. Birog, who had been riding the winds, saw what happened and lifted the baby out of the water and carried him safely back

to his father. Cian was overjoyed, and Lugh was fostered out to a king's daughter, who loved him as if he were her own child.

In his foster home Lugh learnt many skills. Craftsmen taught him to work in wood and metal. Champions and athletes trained him to perform amazing feats. From poets and musicians he heard the stories of the heroes and learnt to play on the harp and timpan. The court physician taught him the use of herbs and elixirs to cure illness, and the magicians revealed to him their secret powers. He grew up as skillful as he was handsome, and when he had learnt every skill that his fosterer could teach him, Lugh made up his mind to go join the king's household. He gathered a group of warriors around him and set off for Tara. As he rode up to the gates of Nuada's Fort Camall, the doorkeeper challenged him.

"Who are you," he asked, "and why have you come here?"

"I am Lugh of the Long Arm," the warrior said, "son of Cian and Eithlinn, and grandson of Balor. Tell the king I want to join his household!"

"No one finds a place in Nuada's household unless he has a special art," said Camall, "so I must ask you what art you have."

"I am master of all the arts," said Lugh. "Go and ask the king if he has in the household any single person who has all the skills. If he has, I will leave these gates and will no longer try to enter Tara."

Camall ran off to take Lugh's message to the king. "Let us see if he is as talented as he claims!" Nuada said. "Bring the chess board out to him and let him compete against our best players."

Lugh played against the best chess players in the land and won every game until there was no one left unbeaten.

Then Nuada said, "Let this young hero in! We have never seen his like before in Tara."

Camall opened the gates, and Lugh entered the fort. He went straight to the hall where Nuada sat surrounded by the most powerful leaders of the Tuatha De Danaan. Lugh passed by them without a word and sat down on the Seat of Wisdom, next to the king. The champions and poets challenged him to a contest of skills, and one by one he outdid them all. Seeing that he possessed the mastery he claimed, the king decided to enlist his aid against Balor and his followers. While Nuada was telling

Lugh about the Fomorian tyranny, another troop of men arrived, as different from Lugh and his followers as night from day. Nuada and his household rose to their feet as soon as they entered, while Lugh looked on in amazement and vexation.

"Why are you rising to your feet for this miserable, hostile rabble when you didn't stand for me?" he cried.

"We must rise," Nuada replied, "or they will kill us all. These are the Fomorians who have come to harry us again!"

Lugh was so furious when he heard this that he drew his sword, rushed at the Fomorians, and killed all but nine of them.

"You should be killed as well!" he told the cringing survivors. "But I'll spare your lives so that you can return to Balor empty-handed and tell him what happened here!"

The terrified messengers fled from Tara and made for the islands of the Fomorians as quickly as they could. When they arrived at Balor's tower and told him about the fate of their companions, his rage was as great as Lugh's.

"Who is this upstart," Balor roared, "who dares to kill my men and send an insulting message back to me?"

His wife, Ceithlinn of the Crooked Teeth, answered him. "I know well who he is from the description these men give of him, and it is bad news for us. He is our own grandson, the son of our daughter, Eithlinn, and he is known as Lugh of the Long Arm. It has been foretold that he will banish the Fomorians from Ireland for all time, and it will be at his hand that you, Balor, will meet your end!"

Balor listened to her, his rage growing with every word. Then he roared, "I'll go to Ireland myself and meet Lugh in battle, and for all his skills, I will overcome my insolent grandson and cut off his head. Then I'll tie that rebellious island to the stern of my ship and tow it back here, and where Ireland once lay there will be empty ocean!"

He marshaled his fearsome army and set out for Ireland.

Meanwhile, Lugh and Nuada had begun to make plans for battle, too, for they knew what Balor would try. They called together all the people who possessed special skills, and Lugh asked each one what contribution he would make toward the struggle.

The magicians told him they would cause the mountains of Ireland to roll toward the Fomorian army, while sheltering the Tuatha De Danaan. The cupbearers promised to bring a great thirst on the Fomorians and then drain the lakes and rivers of Ireland so there would be no water for them to drink, but there would be plenty of water for Nuada's army even if the battle lasted seven years. The smiths, brass-workers, and carpenters swore they would make the strongest spearshafts, swords, and shields. The physician promised to bathe the wounded in a miraculous well so that they would be cured and ready for battle again, and the poet said he would attack the minds of the Fomorians by composing a satirical poem that would cause them to lose heart. Then the Morrigu, the fierce goddess of battlefields, appeared in the shape of a crow. She promised that she would help the Tuatha De Danaan at the hour of their greatest danger and she foretold a victory for them.

"But you must prepare yourself immediately," she said, "for I have seen the warriors of Balor's mighty army stream off the ships at Scetne. They are already marching across Ireland toward Tara!"

Lugh gathered up his troops and filled them full of battle fury. Then the two armies marched toward each other and met on the Plain of Moytura. The Tuatha De Danaan fought fiercely and bravely, but they could not overcome the countless men the Fomorians sent out to meet them. There were heavy losses on both sides, but no side gained the upper hand.

At last the the Fomorians decided to make a final assault. With Ceithlinn at his side, Balor led his army across the plain of Moytura. Helmeted and well-armed, they marched in close formation, men and women side by side.

A great shout went up, and the two armies rushed to meet each other. The battle was fierce and bloody. There was no time now for the physicians to heal the wounded or the smiths to repair weapons. Sword clashed against sword, spears whistled through the air, and battle-axes thudded against shields. The tumult rolled over the Plain of Moytura like thunder, and still they fought on. The river carried away the dead, friend and foe side by side.

At last the two kings met. Balor raised his sword over his head and felled Nuada with one blow. When the Tuatha De Danaan saw this, a groan of despair arose from them, but at that instant the black crow shape of the Morrigu appeared above the battle lines, and fresh courage surged into the Danaan troops.

Lugh rushed to the side of the dying Nuada and angrily taunted Balor. His abuse drove his grandfather into a rage.

"Lift up my eyelid so I can see the gabbling loudmouth who dares insult me like this!" Balor roared. A terrified hush fell over the multitude as ten Fomorian champions pulled on the ropes to raise the heavy lid. Those nearest to Balor fell down to the earth to escape his deadly stare, but Lugh stood his ground, put a stone in his sling, took aim, and let fly directly at Balor's eye as it opened. The force of the stone drove the eye back through Balor's head, and it landed in the midst of the Fomorian lines. Balor fell dead, and hundreds of his followers were killed by the eye's fatal power.

Then Lugh led a last fierce assault against the Fomorians. With the Morrigu hovering above them, they broke through the enemy lines and drove the Fomorians down to the sea, where they boarded their ships in great haste and set sail for their islands, never to return to Ireland.

THE CHILDREN OF LIR

HERE WAS ONCE A KING IN IRELAND CALLED LIR WHO HAD FOUR children, whom he loved dearly. Fionnuala was his eldest child and she looked after her brothers, Aed, Conn, and Fiacra, because their mother had died when the boys were very young. Lir had his dwelling in the north of the country and he and his children lived happily together there until he brought a new wife, Aoife, home to his fort.

Aoife was jealous of Lir's love for his children. Jealousy turned to hatred, and in the end she could bear the sight of them no longer. One morning she told the children they were going to visit their grandfather, Bodb Dearg, king of the Tuatha De Danaan. The younger children were delighted, but Fionnuala was afraid, for she sensed that Aoife was plotting harm.

Halfway to Bodb's fort they reached Lough Derravaragh and halted. Aoife told the children they could bathe in the lake, and the three boys rushed into the water, splashing and shouting, but Fionnuala hung back. When Aoife saw this she ordered the girl to join her brothers, and Fionnuala waded slowly into the lough.

As soon as the children were all together, Aoife took a druid's wand from the folds of her cloak and, pointing at each child in turn, she chanted a spell: "Children of Lir, your good fortune is over! From now on waterfowl will be your family, and your cries will be mingled with the cries of birds."

In an instant, Fionnuala, Aed, Conn, and Fiacra disappeared, and swimming on the lake were four beautiful white swans.

Aoife turned a deaf ear to their pitiful cries and stared unmoved as the frantic creatures thrashed in the water. Fionnuala rushed to the edge of the lake and stretched her long neck toward her stepmother. "Oh, Aoife!" she begged. "Do not condemn us to be swans forever! If you won't give us back our shape, at least put some limit on this enchantment."

Aoife's icy heart melted as she listened to Fionnuala's desperate pleas. "You will not be swans forever!" she cried. "But you must keep the shape of swans for nine hundred years. You will spend three hundred years here on Lough Derravaragh, three hundred years on the Sea of Moyle, and the last three hundred years by the Atlantic Ocean. When a king from the north marries a queen from the south and you hear the sound of a bell pealing out a new faith, you will know that your exile is over. Till then, though you will have the appearance of swans, you will keep your own minds, your own hearts, and your own voices, and your music will be so sweet that it will console all who hear it. But go away from me now, for the very sight of you torments me!" And horrified by her deed, Aoife ran from the shore to the waiting chariot and galloped to Bodb Dearg's fort.

The king was disappointed to find that the children were not with their stepmother, but Aoife had a story ready. "I came alone," she told Bodb Dearg, "because Lir is jealous of your love for his children and he would not let me bring them to your house!"

At first Bodb Dearg was angry at Aoife's words, but then he became suspicious and he sent a message inviting Lir and his children to visit him the next day. Lir was alarmed. At daybreak he set out for Bodb's fort.

From the middle of Lough Derravaragh the swan-children saw the company approaching and recognized their father at the head. They flew to the lakeside and landed there with a clatter of wings, calling out their father's name. Lir heard his children's voices but he could not see them anywhere. He stood puzzled till suddenly, like a blow to the heart, he understood.

"Fionnuala, Aed, Conn, Fiacra! My beloved children! Oh, how can I help you?" he cried out.

"You cannot help us!" Fionnuala called back. "This is Aoife's work. We are doomed to keep this shape for nine hundred years and no power can change that." Seeing the anguish on Lir's face, she longed to comfort him and she began to sing. Her brothers joined in and, as they sang, Lir's desolation faded. Soothed by the music, he and his household fell into a peaceful sleep.

Next morning Lir set off to tell Bodb Dearg the terrible fate of his children. When the king learned of Aoife's treachery, he turned to her in a fury and with his druid's wand he transformed her into a demon of the air. A bitter blast swept her aloft like a withered leaf, and people say that on a stormy night you can still hear Aoife moaning in the wind.

The next day Lir and Bodb Dearg went to Lough Derravaragh, and there they stayed while years became decades, and decades, centuries. Then one day Fionnuala knew it was time for them to leave. As night fell the swans sang Lir and their friends to sleep for the very last time. At daybreak the four swan-children rose into the air, circled the sorrowful crowd below, and set off for the cold Sea of Moyle.

This sea was a stormy band of water between Ireland and Scotland, lashed by gales in spring, by ice and hail in winter. In this desolate place the children suffered such cold that their feathers became brittle as glass, and every spring they were flung from rock to rock by the gales.

One night a fierce storm rose up. Great black thunderclouds piled up and lightning split the sky, and all night long the swans were scattered in the sea spray. When dawn broke, Fionnuala could hardly fly, but she made her way to the Seal's Rock, Carraignarone, and landed. The sun climbed into a clear sky, but Fionnuala could not see her brothers anywhere.

Suddenly Conn appeared, barely clearing the waves. He landed beside Fionnuala, and she put him under her right wing. A while later Fiacra struggled to the rock, and Fionnuala put him under her left wing. At last Aed arrived, beaten and spent, and crept beneath the feathers of Fionnuala's breast. There they rested till their strength returned.

Three hundred years in that stormy sea passed slowly but at last it was time for the swan-children to go.

"And on the way," Fionnuala told her brothers, "we will fly over our home and see our father." They flew over the lovely landscape of their childhood scanning the ground anxiously for Lir's fort. At last they saw the familiar hill, but there was no sign of their father's house. All that remained was a grassy mound, covered with rocks and weeds. The children of Lir landed among the broken earthworks and, as they cowered there, their feathers ruffled by the winds, they remembered their home as they had left it with Aoife on that fateful morning and their hearts nearly cracked with grief. Keening a lament, they rose into the air and headed west to spend the last three hundred years of their exile.

In a quiet inlet on the western coast of Ireland was a small island called Inish Glora, where the swans would shelter. There they sang, and birds flocked from the other western islands to listen to the matchless music.

A new age had dawned in Ireland and the Tuatha De Danaan had been replaced by another race. The old gods had gone underground, and the people now worshiped the Christian god. The children of Lir, themselves, had become legends.

A hermit called Mochaomhog knew the legend. He sensed that the time of the swan-children's release must be close at hand, so he came to Inish Glora and built a church on the island. Every morning as he began to pray, he rang a bronze bell. One calm morning the sound of the bell pealed out across the lake and woke the children of Lir. Fionnuala was overjoyed, for she knew that the bell announced their freedom, and she began to sing.

Hearing her song, the hermit hurried down toward the lake and in the pale morning light he saw the four swans. He called to them across the water: "Children of Lir, don't be afraid! It is for your sake I have come to this island. Come with me and I will help you!"

The children of Lir trusted the hermit and went ashore. Mochaomhog put a silver chain around their necks so that they would never be parted again, and they lived in his hut, happy and peaceful at last.

While the swan-children were living with the hermit, Lairgren, a king from the north, married a queen from the south, and through this marriage the last part of Aoife's spell was broken. The new queen asked for the swans as a marriage gift, so the king traveled to Inish Glora to get them for her. When Mochaomhog refused his request, the angry king seized the chain that linked the swans and dragged the terrified creatures from the hut. They struggled frantically for a moment, then suddenly the tumult stopped. As Lairgren and Mochaomhog watched in horror, the plumage of the swans fell away, and lying on the the ground were four frail old people. Mochaomhog rushed to their side and tried to comfort them. But Fionnuala said to him, "We are dying, my kind friend. Bury us here where we found peace."

Soon after, the children of Lir died peacefully, and Mochaomhog buried them as Fionnuala had requested and raised a stone over their grave.

THE ULSTER CYCLE

onor Mac Nessa was the king of Ulster and he and his followers, the Red Branch Warriors, lived in a large fort at Armagh, in the north of Ireland. Fergus, Conall, and Laoghaire were among the most famous of Conor's champions, but the greatest of them all was Cuchulainn. The druids, judges, and bards of the Ulster court foretold the future and counseled and entertained the king. The women of Ulster, Emer, Deirdre and Levercham, were strong and forceful.

Conor's fort was called Emain Macha. It was given its name by the goddess Macha after a race in which she had been forced to run against Conor's horses although she was pregnant. When her twins were born, Macha gave a loud scream and the strength of all the men who heard it ebbed away. As she died, Macha cursed the Ulstermen, "From this day forward, you will be afflicted by this weakness because of your cruel treatment of me. At the hour of your greatest need, you will become as powerless as I am now and your descendants will be afflicted in the same way for nine generations. My name is Macha and my name and the name of my twins will stick to this place forever."

These prophecies came true. The fort was called Emain Macha, the Twins of Macha. From then on, and for many years, the Ulstermen lay powerless at the time of their greatest need. Cuchulainn was the only man to escape the weakness, and that was because his father, Lugh, like Macha herself, was one of the Tuatha De Danaan. Here are three of my favorite stories from this cycle.

THE BIRTH OF CUCHULAINN

ENTURIES AGO WHEN CONOR MAC NESSA WAS THE KING OF Ulster, a very strange thing happened at his stronghold at Emain Macha. His sister, Dechtire, and her fifty young companions vanished from the fort without a trace. Neither the king nor any members of his household saw them go, and no one knew anything at all about their whereabouts.

Then one day, three years later, a large flock of birds flew across the country and landed at Emain Macha. As Conor and the Red Branch champions watched aghast, the birds ate everything that grew around the fort.

The king could watch the devastation no longer, so he mounted his horse and he and his companions galloped toward the flock. The birds rose into the air, joined together in pairs by silver chains, and flew south across Slieve Fuad, with the king's party following fast behind.

As daylight began to fade, two birds broke away from the flock and headed toward the cluster of Tuatha De Danaan dwellings on the banks of the Boyne River. The king's company followed, but just as they reached the riverbank a heavy shower of snow fell and they lost sight of the birds. Conor ordered his men to find shelter for the night. Bricriu, the poet, set out on this errand, and as he wandered around in the dark, he heard a strange, low noise. He walked in the direction of the sound, and suddenly, out of nowhere, appeared a large, spacious, well-lit house. Bricriu went to the door and looked in. There before him was a handsome couple, a young warrior richly dressed, and at his side, a beautiful woman.

"You are welcome, Bricriu," said the man. When Bricriu heard the warrior call him by name and saw the beauty and splendor of the young man, he knew he was in the presence of Lugh of the Long Arm, one of the most important personages from the land of the Ever Young.

"You are welcome a thousand times over," said the woman at Lugh's side, smiling with delight.

"Why does your wife greet me so warmly?" Bricriu asked.

"It is on her account that I have welcomed you," Lugh replied. "The woman at my side is Dechtire. It was she and her companions who took on the shape of birds and went to Emain Macha to lure Conor and the Ulstermen here."

Bricriu hastened back to tell the news to Conor. The king was delighted when he heard Bricriu's story, and they all hurried to Lugh's mansion. When they arrived Dechtire was not there because she had retired to give birth to a baby, but Lugh gave them a hearty welcome and they settled for the night. In the morning Lugh was gone, but Dechtire and her newborn son sat in the middle of the room, and gathered around her were the fifty girls who had been spirited away from Emain Macha.

The whole company knew that this child, the son of Lugh, was destined to become a great hero, so they took counsel with each other about how he should be raised.

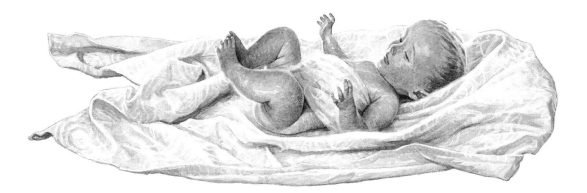

Conor said the child should be fostered to Finnchoem, Dechtire's sister, and Finnchoem was delighted to be chosen. But the other champions objected to this, for they, too, wanted to have a hand in rearing the child.

"We will never be able to judge between ourselves!" said Sencha the Wise. "So let Finnchoem take care of the child until we reach Emain Macha, then Morann can judge between our claims."

Off they set for Ulster and when they arrived there, Morann pronounced the following judgment: "You, Conor, will be his special patron, for he is your sister's child. Finnchoem can feed him, Sencha can make an orator out of him, and Blai can provide for his material needs. Fergus can be like a father to him, and Amergin like a brother. This child is destined for greatness. He will be praised by warriors, sages, and kings. He will be a hero to many. He will be the champion of Ulster and defend her rivers and fords. He will fight her battles and avenge her wrongs!"

Finnchoem and Amergin took the child to Dun Breth to a house made of oak. Dechtire, his mother, married Sualdam Mac Roich, and they helped to rear the child as well. He was guided by his fosterers, who taught him their special arts, and he was given the name Setanta.

When he was six years old, Setanta heard about the boy corps that Conor

Mac Nessa had established at Emain Macha. This group of youths was highly skilled with javelin, spear, and sword, and excelled at games, especially hurling. Setanta was determined to join the troop, so despite his mother's objections he made his way to Emain Macha. At first the boys would not accept him because he was too young, but Setanta proved himself so fierce and fearless that he was allowed to join their ranks.

One day when Setanta was seven, Culann, a smith, came to Emain Macha to offer hospitality to the king. "I am not rich," he told Conor, "I have no lands or inherited wealth. Everything I own I earned myself with my tongs and anvil. I want to honor you by welcoming you to my fort, but I beg you to limit your guests so that I can provide enough food for the feast." So the king picked only the most famous and powerful of his household to go with him to Culann's feast.

Before he set out, Conor went to visit the boy corps in the field, where they were playing games. He arrived in time to see Setanta play against all the 150 boys and beat them. While he watched, they changed to shooting goals. Setanta put every ball past the troop and then, in goal alone, stopped every ball that his companions drove at him.

Finally he wrestled with the whole troop and tumbled them all. Conor was amazed at the boy's prowess and he realized what a great champion Setanta would make. He went over to the boy and said to him, "I'm going to a feast tonight with some of my most prestigious followers. I would like you, Setanta, to come, too, as an honored guest."

"I want to finish the game first," the boy replied. "When I've played enough, I'll follow after you." The king accepted this answer and set off with his followers for Culann's fort.

When they arrived they were greeted by the smith and brought to the hall where the feast had been laid out. Culann said to Conor, "Is all your party present? Or is there someone else still to come?"

"No one," replied the king, forgetting about Setanta.

"Then I'll let loose the hound," the smith said. "He's a savage animal that I got from Spain, and it takes three chains to hold him back, with three men hanging on to each chain. But he guards my stock and cattle well. I'll shut the gate of the enclosure now and let the animal free outside the walls."

The fierce hound was let loose and it made a swift turn around the fortifications of Culann's house. Then it lay down on a hummock, where it could keep watch on the whole place. It crouched there, its giant head on its paws, savage and vigilant, ready to spring.

At Emain Macha, Setanta and the other boys played until it was time to disperse, and then Setanta set out alone for Culann's stronghold. He shortened his journey by hitting the ball with the hurley stick, throwing the stick after the ball, then racing so fast that he caught them both before they fell.

When the monstrous hound saw the boy racing over the green, it let out a bloodcurdling howl that rolled and echoed across the plain. All who heard it froze with horror, but Setanta didn't break his stride. The hound leaped forward, its massive jaws wide open, to tear the child apart.

As it did so, Setanta hurled the ball with all his strength down its gullet, and the force of the throw was so great that it killed the beast.

The hound's savage roar echoed round the hall, and Conor started up in horror. "It's a tragedy that I came here tonight!" he cried out.

"Why is that?" the warriors asked fearfully.

"Because my sister's son was to follow me here. And the roar of that hound is his death knell!"

When the Ulstermen heard this, they rose like one man and stormed out of the fort, swarming over the ramparts in their haste to find the boy. Fastest of all was Fergus Mac Roi, and he was first to reach Setanta.

He found the boy alive, standing over the dead hound, and, overjoyed, he lifted him onto his shoulders and carried him back to Conor. Fergus placed Setanta on the king's knee while all the Red Branch warriors let out shouts of jubilation.

Culann did not join in the rejoicing; he remained outside, looking sadly down at the huge carcass of his hound. Then he came back into the feasting hall and addressed Conor and his retinue.

"It is *indeed* a tragedy that you came here tonight! And it was my bad luck that I invited you at all. I'm glad that you're still alive, boy, but I am ruined! Without the hound to guard it, my fort will be raided and my flocks will be carried off. He saved us all from danger. Little boy, when you killed that hound, you killed my most valued servant!"

"Don't be angry, Culann!" Setanta said. "I'll make up for it!"

"How will you do that, child?" asked Conor.

"I'll find another hound of the same breed and I'll rear him till he can protect Culann as well as the one I've just killed. In the meantime, I will protect your house and herds. I will guard the whole plain and no one will attack you while I am on duty! I will be Culann's hound!"

"That's a fair settlement," said the king.

"No wise man could do better," said Cathbad, the druid. "And from now on, Setanta, your name must be Cuchulainn, the Hound of Culann!"

"I prefer my own name. I'd rather be called Setanta," the boy protested.

"Don't say that," Cathbad replied. "In days to come the name Cuchulainn will be famous throughout Ireland."

And from that moment on the boy was known as Cuchulainn.

BRICRIU'S FEAST

RICRIU, ONE OF THE FOREMOST OF THE ULSTER WARRIORS, WAS famous for causing strife wherever he went. He was such a famous mischief-maker that he got the nickname Bricriu Poison-Tongue.

It came into Bricriu's head to gather together all the Red Branch chiefs at his fort at Dun Rudraige and have some sport with them, so he set about preparing a great feast. He built a dining hall in the same style as the Red Branch hall at Emain Macha, but surpassed it in magnificence. The king's chair, raised on a balcony, was encrusted with jewels that shone so brightly, they turned night into day, and around it were arranged the twelve seats of the twelve tribes of Ulster. Then Bricriu had a platform made for himself on the same level as the king's throne.

When all the preparations had been made, Bricriu went to Emain Macha to invite Conor and the queen to the feast, and also the principal Ulster champions and their wives. Conor told Bricriu that he would accept the invitation but would only go if his followers were willing to attend the feast as well. As it happened the rest of the Ulster chiefs mistrusted Bricriu, and on their behalf Fergus went to Conor to tell him this.

"We don't want to go," Fergus told the king, "for he will set man against man and by nightfall the dead will outnumber the living."

Bricriu overheard what Fergus said to Conor. "It will be worse for you if you don't go!" he said darkly.

"What will happen if we don't go?" Conor asked.

"I will set warrior against warrior until they kill each other."

"We will not be blackmailed by you!" retorted Conor.

"I will set father against son, mother against daughter, wife against wife, till their very mother's milk turns sour!" Bricriu threatened.

"In that case we'd better go!" said Fergus.

Before they set out, Sencha, the judge, called the Ulster chiefs in council to plan how they might protect themselves, and they decided they must get a guarantee from their host that he would leave the hall as soon as the banquet was ready. Bricriu agreed happily.

They had scarcely left Emain Macha, when Bricriu fell to plotting how to cause bad blood among his guests. He drew alongside Laoghaire the Triumphant and greeted him fulsomely. "Laoghaire," he said, "you are a brave warrior. You are the most senior of all the Ulster champions. Why, then, is it that the champion's portion is not given to you at Emain Macha?"

"It would be if I wanted it!" Laoghaire retorted.

"Believe me, the portion *is* worth having! There's a cauldron big enough to hold three men, and I have filled it with strong wine. By way of food I have a seven-year-old boar that has been fed from birth of the best: fresh milk and fine meal in springtime, curds and sweet milk in the summer, nuts and harvest wheat in autumn, and beef broth during the winter. As well as the boar, there is a seven-year-old bull that has eaten only the sweetest meadow hay and oats. Also a hundred honey-soaked wheat cakes, with a quarter bushel of wheat in each one. And it should all be yours, Laoghaire!"

"It had better be mine or there'll be blood spilt!" Laoghaire exclaimed. And Bricriu went off laughing.

A little while later Bricriu drew close to Conall Cearnach and gave him the same advice. When he felt confident that Conall would fight for his right to the champion's portion, Bricriu made his way to Cuchulainn's side.

"How can anyone deny the hero's portion to you, Cuchulainn? You are the acknowledged champion and darling of Ulster. You have defended her borders. You have fought her enemies single-handed. Everyone knows your achievements surpass theirs, so why is the portion not yours by right?"

As he listened to Bricriu, Cuchulainn grew angrier by the minute. "I swear by the gods of my tribe I'll take the head of anyone who dares to claim the portion ahead of me!" he muttered grimly. Then Bricriu left Cuchulainn and mingled with his guests until they reached Dun Rudraige.

When they arrived there the Ulster visitors settled into their quarters, Conor and his men on one side of the building, the queen and the chieftains' wives on the other. Then they made their way to the banqueting hall, where musicians and players entertained the visitors. When the meal was ready to be served, the host and his wife took leave of their guests as agreed, but at the door of the hall Bricriu turned to the assembly. "The champion's portion is over there!" he announced. "Only the greatest hero deserves it. Make sure it goes to the right man!" With that the couple climbed up to the glass viewing room above the hall.

"Bring the hero's portion to Cuchulainn, where you all know it belongs!" roared Cuchulainn's charioteer. Laoghaire and Conall sprang to their feet and seized their weapons. "He doesn't deserve it," they shouted and leapt across the room to fight. Cuchulainn defended himself fiercely with his sword and shield. The melee was so violent that one half of the hall blazed like the sun, lit by the sparks from their swords, while the other half was covered in the enamel dust that fell like snow from their shields.

At last, Sencha the judge stood up. "Stop!" he roared above the din. "Two men against one is shameful!" Conall and Laoghaire put down their weapons.

"I'll settle this dispute," Sencha said. "Will you abide by my judgment?"

"We will," agreed the three champions.

"Then the champion's portion will be divided among the whole company tonight, and some other time we will decide who is the greatest of the Ulster heroes."

Peace was restored, and the food and wine was divided equally among all.

Watching these developments from the balcony, Bricriu was dismayed to find his feast proceeding harmoniously and decided it was time to set woman against woman as he had set man against man. He went down and waited outside the door for the women to come out of the hall. First out was Fidelma, the wife of Laoghaire, and Bricriu went down to her side.

"I'm the lucky man tonight to meet someone as distinguished as you, Fidelma!" he said. "The wife of Laoghaire and the daughter of Conor Mac Nessa, the king himself! By virtue of birth, beauty, and intelligence you should take second place to none. I'll let you in on a secret! When the women are returning to the feast, if you are the first to reenter the hall you will be considered first in rank among the Ulster women from now on." Fidelma was flattered and pleased.

Just then Lendabar, wife of Conall, came out of the hall, and Bricriu flattered her and told her the same story.

Finally Bricriu greeted Emer, Cuchulainn's wife, and spoke effusively of her lineage, her beauty, and her learning and of her unquestionable right to be the first lady in Ulster after the queen herself. His blandishment and flattery reached new heights, as did his pleasure, when he noted Emer's determination to be first back in the hall.

The three noblewomen and their retinues strolled about companionably in the evening air beyond the third of the ridges that encircled the feasting hall, each one confident that Bricriu had spoken to her alone. When the time came to return to the feast, they began to walk in step toward the hall. At the third ridge, their progress was stately and serene. By the time they reached the second ridge, their steps had become shorter and quicker. At the

first ridge, all dignity was abandoned and the women hitched their skirts around their waists and ran at full tilt, each one trying to be first through the door.

The clamor that the women made resounded through the hall. The men inside sprang for their weapons, striking at each other in their befuddlement, till Sencha called them to order.

"Stop, put down your swords! This is not the arrival of an army that you hear! These are your own women! This is Bricriu's work. He has set your wives against each other while they were out taking the air. If he gets inside with the women, there will be trouble. Shut the door quickly!"

The doorkeeper slammed the door just as Emer, the fastest of the women, arrived. She shouted to be let in first because she had won the race and deserved a higher place than Lendabar or Fidelma. When they heard Emer say this, Conall and Laoghaire ran to the door to open it for their wives so that they might secure a place above Emer. Conor was alarmed at the prospect of another fight and he ordered the champions to return to their places. When the company was calm again, Sencha told them that it would be a war of words that would settle the matter, not a war of arms.

So outside the door, each wife in turn praised her husband's character and person and paid tribute to his courage, skill, deeds, lineage, and virtue, all of them hoping to out-praise the others. When the three warriors heard their wives praising them in such glowing terms, each was determined that his spouse would be the first to enter the hall and claim the highest rank. Laoghaire and Conall hacked at the wall with their swords to force an entrance for their wives, but Cuchulainn simply wrenched one side of the hall up by the foundations and held it so high that the stars in the sky were visible, and Emer stepped into the hall first. Then Cuchulainn let the building fall with a mighty crash, and the foundations sank seven feet into the ground. Bricriu's balcony dipped and slipped, and he and his wife slid out of it and landed among the hounds in the ditch below. When Bricriu saw his house listing at a crazy angle, he ran inside to protest, but he was in such disarray and so caked with mud that no one recognized him until he started to harangue them.

Though Bricriu had paid dearly for his mischief on this occasion, he had succeeded in sowing the seeds of dissension among the Red Branch heroes, and the quarrel about the champion's portion came up again and again. The three contenders went through many tests and ordeals, and the struggle for succession raged on until it was resolved in a bloody and terrifying way.

One evening Conor and Fergus were presiding over a feast in Emain Macha. Laoghaire was there, but Conall and Cuchulainn were absent. As the feast was ending and darkness was drawing in, a giant figure appeared at the end of the hall. He was a monstrous creature and he terrified the assembly as he lumbered across the room. His yellow eyes were as big as cauldrons, and each finger was as thick as a man's wrist. He wore an old skin tunic and over it a rough brown cloak. In one hand, he carried a cudgel the size of a mature tree, and in the other, an ax so sharp that it sliced the hairs that floated in the wind.

"I have come on a mission," said the giant, "for I know that the Ulstermen are world-famous for their courage, dignity, and magnanimity. I have traveled the world through Africa, Europe, and Asia. But I haven't found a man who will do what I ask, not in Greece, Scythia, or Spain. Will anyone here do what I ask?"

"What is your quest?" Conor asked.

"To find a man who will make a pact with me and keep his word."

"That shouldn't be hard!" the king exclaimed.

"Harder than you think," the giant said, "because I'm looking for a man who will agree to cut off my head tonight and let me cut off his head tomorrow." There was silence in the room.

"Conor and Fergus are exempt because of their status as kings," the giant went on, "but is there anyone else present who will make this pact with me?" Still no one spoke. The giant sighed. "Just as I expected! Where are those who claim the champion's portion? Won't one of those heroes pledge his word? Where is Laoghaire the Triumphant?"

"Here I am!" Laoghaire roared. "And I accept your challenge. Bend down and put your neck on the block! I'll cut off your head!"

"That's easily said, but what about tomorrow night?" asked the giant.

"I'll be here," promised Laoghaire.

The huge man bent down, and with one blow of the ax, Laoghaire cut off his head, burying the blade in the block. A torrent of blood flowed across the floor and the head rolled against the wall. Then, to the horror of the crowd, the giant rose, gathered up his head, his axe, and his block and, holding them against his chest, walked out of the room.

The following night, as darkness fell, the giant returned to Emain Macha. His head was back in place, and in his hand he held his cudgel, ax, and block. He stared around the room looking for Laoghaire, but Laoghaire was nowhere to be seen. The giant let out a great resigned sigh and issued his challenge once again. This time it was Conall who agreed to the pact. He gave his solemn word that he would be there on the following night, took up the ax and, with one swift stroke, severed the giant's head from the body.

Once more the giant picked up his head and departed.

The next evening, when the giant returned to Red Branch banquet hall, a great crowd had gathered, but Conall was not among them. The giant laughed contemptuously. "Ulstermen, you're no better that the rest for all your talk!" he jeered. Then he spied Cuchulainn in the middle of the throng. "What about the fierce Cuchulainn, the Hound of Ulster?" he roared. "Can he keep a bargain?"

"I want no bargain with you!" Cuchulainn shouted, and he grabbed the ax from the giant's hand and struck off his head with such force that it bounced to the ceiling. When it landed, Cuchulainn took another crack, but still the giant rose to his feet, took up his shattered head, and left.

On the fourth evening every warrior in Ulster was in the Red Branch hall to see if Cuchulainn would be there. Cuchulainn was indeed present, but he was dejected and frightened and would not speak to anyone.

Suddenly the giant appeared at the far end of the hall. "Where is Cuchulainn?" he demanded.

"Here I am," Cuchulainn answered in a low voice.

"You haven't as much to say for yourself tonight!" mocked the giant. "I can see you are scared to die! But at least you have kept your word." The giant pointed to the block, and Cuchulainn knelt down and laid his head on it.

"Stretch out your neck!" the giant ordered.

"Kill me quickly and don't torment me," Cuchulainn begged.

"Your neck is too short for the block!"

"Then I'll make it as long as a heron's neck!" Cuchulainn cried and he distorted his body and stretched his neck till it reached across the block. Using both hands, the giant swung the ax so high that it struck the rafters. The swish of his cloak through the air and the hiss of the ax as it came down sounded through the hall like the wind through trees on a stormy night. As the crowd watched helplessly, the ax swung down toward Cuchulainn's neck, but it was the blunt side of the blade that landed there and it came down so gently that it hardly marked the skin.

"Stand up, Cuchulainn!" the giant said. "You are the champion of Ulster. No one is your equal for bravery and honor. From now on your supremacy must go unchallenged. You must be awarded the champion's portion, and your wife must take first place after the queen in the banqueting hall. I am Cu Roi and I swear by the oath of my people that whomever disputes this puts his life in danger!" With that, the giant disappeared.

DEIRDRE OF THE SORROWS

 N IRELAND, LONG AGO, EVERY CHIEFTAIN'S HOUSEHOLD HAD its own bard who entertained the company with songs and poetry and praised the heroic deeds of his master. The bards in turn were held in high esteem, and Felimid, the bard of the king of Ulster, held an important place within the clan.

One day Felimid invited the king to his house and prepared a lavish feast in his honor. The guests ate and drank their fill, and the hall was full of the sounds of entertainment. Felimid's wife oversaw the feast, moving among the guests the whole night long, until at last they began to fall asleep. Then she made her way to her own room, for her baby was about to be born. As she passed through the house, the child in her womb gave a shriek so loud that the warriors seized their weapons and rushed to see what had made the unearthly cry. Nobody could say what it was till Felimid came from his wife's chamber and told them.

Then Felimid's wife emerged distraught and frightened. She turned to Cathbad the Druid and said, "You are a wise and generous man, and you can foretell the future. Can you please tell me what lies inside my womb?"

The druid answered, "The infant that screamed from your womb is a girl. She will grow up to be a beautiful woman. She will have shining eyes and long, heavy, fair hair. Her pale skin will be flushed with pink, her lips will be as red as strawberries, and she will have teeth like pearls. Queens will envy her, and kings will desire her. She will be known as Deirdre of the Sorrows, and because of her, there will be great anguish in Ulster!"

"Kill the child," the warriors shouted, "so that Ulster may be spared!"

But Conor Mac Nessa held up his hand. "No!" he said, "I will take this child and foster her to someone I trust, and when she grows up she will be my wife."

No one dared argue with the king. He built a fort for Deirdre in a lonely place, and she grew more beautiful each day. But apart from the king himself, the only people to see her beauty were her foster father and Levercham, her nurse.

One winter's day Deirdre's foster father was slaughtering a calf for veal and the blood flowed out across the snow. As Deirdre watched from her window a raven swooped down to sip the blood. Deirdre turned to Levercham and said, "I could love a man like that, a man with hair as black as a raven and skin like the snow and cheeks as red as blood!"

"Good luck is yours," Levercham answered, "for not far from here lives such a man. He is called Naoise, and he is one of the sons of Usnach. These three brothers are so courageous and skillful that, back to back, they can hold off all the warriors in Ulster. They are so swift that they can take down deer like hunting dogs. And when they sing together their song is so harmonious that women and men, entranced by the music, fall silent. Ardan, Ainnle, and Naoise, these are their names, but Naoise is the strongest and most handsome of the three."

"If that is so," said Deirdre, "I will not have a day's good health till I see him!"

Not long after this, when spring had come to Emain Macha, Deirdre heard melodious singing coming from the ramparts of the fort. She stole out, for she knew that it must be Naoise. She walked past him without glancing in his direction, but Naoise saw her, and was so struck by her beauty, that he stopped in the middle of his song and he shouted out, "This is a fine young lassie passing me by!"

"Lasses are bound to be fine when there are no lads about!" Deirdre retorted.

"You have the king for yourself!" said Naoise, realizing that the beautiful girl must be Deirdre.

Deirdre looked at Naoise. "If I had my choice between a fine young fellow like yourself and an old man like Conor, I would settle for you!"

"But you are promised to the king," said Naoise. "And don't forget what Cathbad has prophesied about you!"

"Are you turning me down?" Deirdre shouted.

"I am indeed!" replied Naoise.

In a fit of passion, Deirdre ran up to Naoise and, grabbing his head between her hands, she cried, "May dishonor and disgrace fall on this head unless you take me away with you!"

Naoise was stricken with dread when he heard these words and realized that Deirdre had put a *geis*, a most solemn bond, on him. He knew that to disobey that *geis* would bring about his downfall, so, terrified as he was of Conor Mac Nessa's anger, he knew he must take Deirdre with him. That night, as darkness fell, Deirdre and the sons of Usnach fled from the province of Ulster.

For a while they wandered around Ireland going from one king's protection to another's, but they were harried again and again by Conor's men. In the end, they could stand it no longer and left Ireland for Scotland.

There they set up camp among the wild mountains and glens and lived on the game they caught. When winter came and the game was scarce, they stole cattle for food. These cattle raids angered the people of the place, who marched on Naoise's compound to kill him and his followers. The sons of Usnach, seeing the men advance, fled to the king of Scotland and offered to fight for him in exchange for food and sanctuary. The king was glad to have such fine soldiers as allies and took them into his service. Because they remembered Cathbad's warning that Deirdre's beauty would bring about death and destruction, Naoise and his followers built their houses in a circle with a secret house for Deirdre in the center.

But early one morning the king's steward rose and stole into the brothers' quarters. There he found the secret hut and Naoise and Deirdre asleep in it. Like everyone else who saw her, he was mesmerized by the girl's beauty and he ran in great excitement to tell the king.

"Until this day we have never found anyone worthy to be your queen, but now I have found a woman worthy to be queen of the whole world! Kill Naoise while he's still asleep and make the woman your wife!"

"I won't do that," the king said. "We'll try a different way. Every day when Naoise is out, go to the girl's room and tell her that the king of Scotland loves her. Ask her to leave Naoise and come here to be my wife." So every day, in secret, the steward wooed Deirdre for the king and every night when Naoise returned, Deirdre told him the whole story.

Then the king arranged dangerous missions for the three brothers, hoping that they would be killed, but their skill and bravery brought them through unharmed. At last the king gave Deirdre an ultimatum: Either she come to him voluntarily, or she would be taken by force and the three brothers killed.

Deirdre warned Naoise of the danger. "We must leave immediately," she urged, "or by nightfall tomorrow you and your brothers will be dead!" That night, the whole party stole away in boats and headed for a remote island from where they could see both Ireland and Scotland. When the news reached Ireland, the Red Branch warriors went to Conor. "This is Deirdre's

doing, not theirs," they told him. "It would be tragic if the sons of Usnach were killed in a foreign land because of a headstrong woman. You should forgive them."

"Let them come back, then," the king said, "and tell them I will send someone to guarantee their safe passage."

The fugitives were delighted. They sent a message back to Conor thanking him for his pardon and requesting him to send the champions Fergus, Dubhtach, and Cormac. Conor agreed to this, but there was treachery in his heart. He still wanted Deirdre for himself.

Conor knew that there was a geis on Fergus that he must never, under pain of death, refuse to attend a feast that had been prepared in his honor, and he used that knowledge to trick Fergus. He ordered him to bring Deirdre, Naoise, and their household directly to Emain Macha as soon as they arrived in Ireland and on no account to eat or drink anywhere until they had eaten and drunk with him. Then he ordered Borrach, a chief whose

house lay on the route to Emain Macha, to prepare a feast in Fergus's honor. When Fergus arrived at Borrach's stronghold, the chieftain did as the king had ordered and invited him to the feast. At first Fergus declined the invitation, but when Borrach assured him that the feast was in his honor and reminded him of his geis, Fergus turned pale. "It is a cruel choice!" he shouted. "I have given my word to accompany Naoise and Deirdre to Emain Macha without delay but I cannot refuse your hospitality, unwelcome as it is!"

Naoise and Deirdre were alarmed. "Are you forsaking us for a meal?"

"I'm not forsaking you," Fergus said, "but I cannot betray my geis. I'll send my son, Fiacha, with you to ensure your safe conduct." So Deirdre and the sons of Usnach set off for Emain Macha while Fergus, Cormac, and Dubtach went to Borrach's feast.

When the travelers arrived at Emain Macha another band of visitors was already with Conor. They were led by Eogan, whose father, the king of Fernmag, had been a long-standing enemy of Conor's. Eogan had come to make peace with the king of Ulster, and Conor, seizing his chance, had accepted his offer on condition that he kill the sons of Usnach.

As Deirdre and the brothers stood on the green at the center of Emain Macha, Eogan of Fernmag began to move toward the sons of Usnach. Fergus's son, Fiacha, sensing danger, went up to stand beside Naoise. As Eogan came close, Naoise went to greet him. In reply, Eogan drew his sword and drove it through Naoise's body. As Naoise fell, Fiacha caught him in his arms and pulled him down to shield him with his body, but Eogan killed Naoise through the body of Fiacha.

Then Conor's mercenaries closed in on Ainnle, Ardan, and their followers. They hunted them like hares from one end of the green to the other and killed them all. Deirdre was seized, her hands were tied behind her back, and she was handed over to Conor.

When Fergus heard of Conor's treachery he was mad with anger, and for sixteen years, he and his allies made raids on Conor Mac Nessa's territory. In revenge, Deirdre was kept in Conor's house for a year. In all that time she was never once seen to smile or laugh. She hardly slept at all, and the little food she ate barely kept her alive.

When Conor brought musicians to play for her, she would not listen to their songs. Instead she raised her voice and recited a poem lamenting Naoise's death. When the king tried to win her favor, she accused him bitterly of Naoise's murder and threw his love back in his face. Conor grew more and more enraged at Deirdre's defiance and at her rejection of him.

One day when Eogan was visiting Emain Macha, Conor brought him to see Deirdre. Then the king asked her. "Of all that you see, Deirdre, what do you hate most?"

"I hate you, Conor, and I hate Eogan who killed Naoise," Deirdre answered.

"In that case you can spend a year with him as well!" said Conor, and he handed her over to Eogan.

The next day the three of them drove out to the fair at Emain Macha. Deirdre was in the chariot between Eogan and Conor and throughout the journey she kept her eyes fixed on the ground, for she had vowed that she would not look at either of the men. Seeing this, Conor taunted her. "Well, Deirdre, here you are where you can eye us both, like a ewe between two rams!"

They were galloping past a huge boulder when Conor spoke these mocking words, and hearing them, Deirdre could bear her fate no longer. She leapt out of the chariot to escape her tormentors, fell against the rock, and died.

THE FINN CYCLE

ong ago, a band of men called the Fianna roamed through Ireland. This troop was made up of the noblest, bravest, swiftest, strongest, most honorable men in the land. From November to May, the Fianna were the soldiers of the king. They kept the country safe from pirates and invaders and punished public enemies at home. In the summer months, they received no pay, but lived off the land, fishing and hunting for food and selling the skins of animals.

To be accepted as one of the Fianna, a man had to obey certain rules and prove himself in trials of strength, bravery, and skill. He had to swear to be loyal to his leader, to respect all women, and to help the poor. He had to study the art of poetry so he could compose his own poems and memorize traditional rhymes and stories. When he had pledged all these things, his comrades-in-arms tested his courage and skill. If he came through these trials as a bravehearted warrior, a lightfooted hunter, and an eloquent poet, he was allowed to join the company.

The captain of the Fianna had great power and sat next to the king at the banquet table. Finn Mac Cumhaill of Clan Bascna was the most famous leader of them all, and during his time, they had a heyday of such glory that the stories of their adventures were told all over Ireland from that day on.

FINN AND THE SALMON OF KNOWLEDGE

ONG AGO IN IRELAND, A DRUID LIVED ON THE HILL OF Allen in Leinster, in a shining, white-fronted fort called Almu. His name was Tadg and he had a daughter, Muirne, who was so beautiful that the sons of kings and chiefs came in great numbers to ask for her hand. Among her suitors was Cumhaill, head of Clan Bascna and leader of the Fianna. Cumhaill asked Tadg for permission to marry his daughter again and again, but each time he was refused. In spite of these refusals Cumhaill was determined to have Muirne for his wife, so he entered the fort of Almu and carried her off.

When the druid heard that his daughter had been abducted, he was furious and went directly to the king and complained bitterly. Conn sent messengers to Cumhaill ordering him to send Muirne back to her father, but Cumhaill refused. He told the king that he would give him anything he asked, anything at all, except Muirne. When Conn heard this defiant reply, he gathered together from the east and the west the chiefs and soldiers of Clan Morna, the great rivals of Clan Bascna. From the south, bands of men loyal to Clan Bascna marched to Leinster to help Cumhaill. The two armies met at Cnuca, near Castleknock, and a fierce battle ensued. Cumhaill fought bravely leading his small force against Conn's bigger army, but he was overpowered and killed, and only a few of his men escaped alive. After the battle the king rewarded the leader of Clan Morna by putting him at the head of the Fianna.

When Muirne heard that her husband had been killed in battle and his followers scattered, she went back to Almu to seek refuge with her father, but Tadg was so angry with her for eloping with Cumhaill that he turned her away from his door. Muirne made her way to the king's fortress at Tara and asked Conn for his protection, not only from Clan Morna, but from her father as well. The king took pity on her, and one of his servants brought her to a kinsman's house, where she was kept in hiding. Not long afterward she gave birth to a boy, the son of Cumhaill, and she called him Demne.

While he was a baby, Demne had no home where he could be safe. Goll Mac Morna, the new leader, was determined to kill him for he was afraid that Cumhaill's son would claim his position as leader of the Fianna when he grew up. Muirne knew that her son was in danger while he was with her, so, with a sad heart, she handed him over to two of her trusted women attendants, skilled trackers who had been trained to survive in the wilderness.

As soon as Muirne's servants were given the baby, they took him away with them, and hid with him in the woods and valleys of Slieve Bloom. There they guarded him closely and reared him and and cared for him as if he were their own child. Muirne slipped away out of the territory controlled by Clan Morna and settled in the south of the country.

Six years after she had parted with her child, Muirne came secretly to visit Demne in his forest hideout. She wanted to see her son again and make sure he was hidden from his enemies and well cared for by his friends. Demne lived in a hunting bothy made of wattle and mud and roofed with branches, so that it was almost invisible in the depths of the wood, but Muirne found it and went in. Her two women servants recognized her and welcomed her joyfully. They led her into the room where her fair-haired son lay asleep. She lifted him up and, holding him close, hugged him and talked to him. Then rocking him in her arms she sang him a lullaby until he went back to sleep. When he was sound asleep, Muirne whispered good-bye to her son and went out of the room. She thanked the faithful women for the love and protection they were giving her child and asked them to look after him until he was old enough to fend for himself. Then she stole away, slipping from wood to wilderness till she reached the safety of her own territory.

As Demne grew up, his guardians taught him to love the changing seasons and life in the woods and hills around him, and he grew up out of doors, hardy in winter and carefree in summer. He became a skillful tracker and hunter; he could outstrip the hare, and bring down a stag on his own without the help of a deerhound, and he could make a wild duck drop from the sky with one stone from a sling.

As he became more and more adventurous, Demne went farther and farther afield, in spite of the warnings of his guardians, and before long word came to Goll Mac Morna of a fair-haired forest boy. One day Demne came out of the woods onto the playing green of a large fort. There were boys playing hurley on the green, and Demne joined in the game and was by far the best player of them all. As soon as the game was over, he disappeared into the forest so swiftly the boys scarcely saw him go. The next day he came back, and on his own, played against a quarter of the boys and won. Again he slipped away. The next day, a third of the boys measured themselves against him, but Demne still beat them. Finally they were all ranged against him, but the fair-haired stranger took the ball from them all and won the game.

"What is your name?" the boys asked.

"Demne," he said, and turned away and disappeared into the forest. The boys told the chieftain who owned the fort about the stranger who had beaten them all single-handed.

"Surely among the lot of you, you should be able to beat one boy!" the chieftain said mockingly. "Did he tell you his name?"

"He said his name was Demne."

"And what does this champion look like?"

"He's tall and well-built and his hair is very fair."

"Then we'll give him the nickname Finn because of that white hair," said the chieftain, and from that day on Finn, which means "fair-haired," became Demne's name.

The chieftain's son grew
jealous of Finn's strength and skill
and he turned his companions against
the newcomer. When Finn arrived the next day
ready for a game, instead of playing with him, all the
boys flung their hurley sticks at him. Finn grabbed one of the
hurleys from the ground and made a run at the boys, knocking seven
of them to the ground and scattering the rest. Then he escaped to the
shelter of the forest.

The two women who had guarded Demne so faithfully knew they
could keep him safe no longer, now that tales of his exploits were on
everyone's lips.

"You must leave us, Finn. The Mac Morna scouts will be on your track,
and if they find you, they will kill you," they told him.

Finn sadly said good-bye to his brave guardians and headed out, away
from the dangerous terrain of Slieve Bloom. He traveled south, slipping
stealthily through bogs and woods down the country until he reached
Lough Lene in Kerry.

He made
his way to the stronghold
of the king of Bantry and joined his band of fighters
and trackers, but he told no one his name or lineage. Before long, it was
clear to all that the newcomer had no equal as a hunter, and was a skilled
chess player as well. The king observed the young man closely and saw in
his face a resemblance to Cumhaill, his father.

"Who are you?" he demanded.

"I'm called Demne," replied Finn.

"No, you are not! You're the son of Cumhaill. You are called Finn Mac Cumhaill, and your mother was Muirne, the druid's daughter. Goll Mac Morna killed your father at Castleknock and now he is out to kill you, too! Leave my place at once. I can't protect you!"

So once again Finn was a fugitive, and he decided to seek refuge with his uncle Crimhall. Finn felt safe in the company of loyal kinsmen, and he listened closely to the old man's stories about Cumhaill and the Fianna. As Crimhall told him about their bravery in battle, their skill in the hunt, and their mastery of the art of poetry, Finn made up his mind to overthrow Goll Mac Morna and take his hereditary place at the head of the Fianna. But he knew that he must gather around him a band of men. He knew, too, that he would not be considered worthy to take command of the Fianna until he was as fine a poet as he was a warrior and hunter.

Now there was a poet and teacher called Finnegas who lived near the river Boyne, and Finn decided to learn the art of poetry from this wise man. Finnegas had spent seven years camping near a pool on the river Boyne because the red-speckled Salmon of Knowledge lived in this pool and it had been foretold that whoever ate one of these fish would possess an understanding of everything in the world, past, present, and future. The salmon had eaten the berries that fell from a magic rowan tree overhanging the pool, and from the berries they had absorbed all the wisdom of the world.

When Finn arrived at Finnegas's hut, the poet had just caught one of the salmon and knew that, at last, all the knowledge of the world would be his.

Finnegas gave the fish to Finn and ordered him to cook it, but he gave the youth a solemn warning not to taste even the smallest morsel. Finn

made a fire and cooked the salmon, but as he lifted it off the spit, the charred skin of the fish seared his thumb. The burn made Finn wince, and he stuck his blistered thumb into his mouth to ease the pain. Then he brought the fish to Finnegas. As Finn handed him the fish, the poet looked closely at his pupil and saw a change in him.

"Are you sure you didn't taste the salmon?" he asked the boy anxiously.

"No," said Finn, "but I burnt my thumb on the skin of the fish and put it in my mouth to soothe it."

"What is your name?" the poet cried.

"My name is Demne," the boy replied.

"Your name is Finn!" said the poet sadly. "As mine is too. It was prophesied that a fair-haired man would eat the Salmon of Knowledge, and you are that fair-haired one, not me! So the eternal knowledge is yours now, not mine. You may as well eat the whole fish, Finn!"

So Finn ate the Salmon of Knowledge and from that moment on when he put his thumb in his mouth, whatever he needed to know was revealed to him.

Finn stayed with Finnegas on the banks of the Boyne, learning the art of poetry, and to prove that he had mastered that difficult art, he composed his first poem in praise of early summer, the season he loved best of all.

SUMMER

EARLY SUMMER, loveliest season,
THE WORLD IS BEING COLORED IN.
WHILE DAYLIGHT LASTS ON THE HORIZON,
SUDDEN, THROATY BLACKBIRDS SING.

THE DUSTY-COLORED CUCKOO CUCKOOS.
"WELCOME, SUMMER" IS WHAT HE SAYS.
WINTER'S UNIMAGINABLE.
THE WOOD'S A WICKERWORK OF BOUGHS.

SUMMER MEANS THE RIVER'S SHALLOW,
THIRSTY HORSES NOSE THE POOLS.
LONG HEATHER SPREADS OUT ON BOG PILLOWS.
WHITE BOG COTTON DROOPS IN BLOOM.

SWALLOWS SWERVE AND FLICKER UP.
MUSIC STARTS BEHIND THE MOUNTAIN.
THERE'S MOSS AND A LUSH GROWTH UNDERFOOT.
SPONGY MARSHLAND GLUGS AND STUTTERS.

BOG BANKS SHINE LIKE RAVENS' WINGS.
THE CUCKOO KEEPS ON CALLING WELCOME.
THE SPECKLED FISH JUMPS; AND THE STRONG
SWIFT WARRIOR IS UP AND RUNNING.

A LITTLE, JUMPY, CHIRPY FELLOW
HITS THE HIGHEST NOTE THERE IS;
THE LARK SINGS OUT HIS CLEAR TIDINGS.
SUMMER, SHIMMER, PERFECT DAYS.

THE ENCHANTED DEER

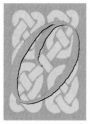NE FINE DAY WHEN FINN MAC CUMHAILL AND HIS MEN were returning home after a day's hunting, a beautiful deer started up in front of them and began to run as fast as the wind toward the fort of Almu. The doe ran with such speed that she outstripped the hunting party, and one by one the men and their dogs fell back exhausted. But Finn and his two hounds kept up the chase. As they swept along the side of a valley, the deer was still in view but she was outstripping Bran and Sceolan, the swiftest dogs in the pack, and Finn knew he would never be able to overtake her. Suddenly, in full flight, she stopped and lay down on the smooth grass. Finn was amazed at this strange behavior and he ran on toward her, Bran and Sceolan ahead of him. When Finn came close to the beautiful doe he was even more astonished to see his two fierce deerhounds frolicking around her, licking her face and neck and patting her limbs.

Finn knew by this that no harm should come to the deer, so he called his dogs to heel and they set off for the Hill of Allen, where Almu stood. After they had walked a little distance Finn looked behind him, and there, on their heels, was the doe following them home. When they reached the fort, Finn and his hounds went through the entrance, and their strange companion followed them. Everyone knew then that this was no ordinary deer, and she was given safe quarters for the night.

After the evening meal Finn retired to his room. Just as he lay down, a lovely woman walked in, dressed in clothes of the finest material, richly ornamented with gold. Finn stared at the visitor in surprise, for he knew she was not a member of the household, and in admiration, because she was so beautiful. Then the woman spoke.

"I am the doe you and your hounds spared this evening and brought safe-ly back to Almu. I am called Sadb. A druid of the Tuatha De Danaan, the Dark Druid, changed me into a deer because I refused his love. For three years now I have endured the hardship and danger of a wild deer's life in a part of Ireland far away from here. In the end, one of the druid's servants took pity and told me that if I could get inside a Fianna fortress, the druid's power over me would come to an end. I have been running through the woods of Ireland without stopping so that I could come close to the Hill of Allen, for I knew you were the leader of the Fianna. I outran your hunting party until Bran and Sceolan were my only pursuers. Then I stopped, for I knew they wouldn't kill me. They recognized my true nature, which is like their own."

Finn was moved by the woman's story and by her gentleness and beauty, and he fell deeply in love with her. For months he abandoned all his former activities and was not seen at any hunt, fight, or feast. Instead he stayed with his beloved Sadb and he gave her a pet name, the Flower of Almu.

But word came to Almu from the king, who needed Finn's help to drive invaders out of Dublin Bay, so Finn had to leave Almu and beautiful Sadb.

For seven days Finn was away, driving back the Lochlann from the Irish coast. The moment the battle was over, he hurried back to the Hill of Allen.

When the shining walls of Almu came into view, his eyes scoured the ramparts for his first glimpse of Sadb. He came closer and closer, his eyes

straining anxiously to see his wife, but there was no sign of her anywhere.

Instead of Sadb, his servants came out to meet him. They cheered his safe return, but their faces were sad.

"Where is Sadb?" Finn cried out. No one spoke, for no one wanted to be the first to break the bad news. "Where is my wife?" Finn asked again.

"Don't blame us, Finn!" his servants implored. "While you were away fighting the invaders, you appeared here outside the fort with Bran and Sceolan at your heels. You put the pipes to your lips, and its humming music filled Almu, mesmerizing and soothing us all. Sadb, your gentle wife, at once came running out of her room, thinking you had returned. She flew down through the pass and out toward the gates of Almu. By then we knew that it was not you who was blowing the pipes, but someone who had assumed your shape, but Sadb ignored our entreaties. 'I must go out to greet Finn! He has saved and protected me! And now I am carrying his child.' We begged her to stay inside the fort, but she ran out of Almu and threw herself into the arms of the one who had taken on your shape. Immediately she realized her mistake. She gave a wild shriek and drew back, but the sorcerer struck her with a wand. In an instant Sadb was gone, and a beautiful, frightened deer stood in her place. The doe stood trembling on the plain, looking back piteously toward Almu. Then the druid's two hounds, barking wildly, chased the terrified deer away from the fort. Three or four times she made

desperate efforts to spring back across the fortifications, but each time the hounds seized her by the throat and pulled her back.

"Oh, Finn!" they cried, seeing the grief and horror on his face. "We swear to you that we tried our best to save Sadb. Before you could count to twenty we had snatched our spears and swords and rushed out to the plain to rescue her, but the plain was deserted. We could see nothing, no sign of woman or deer, man or hound. Nothing! But we could hear the beat of running feet drumming the plain, and the howl of dogs. These sounds filled the air all around us and bewildered us, for each of us heard the sounds coming from a different direction."

Finn threw his head back in anguish when he heard this and hammered his breast with his fists. He uttered not one word but went alone to his quarters, and there he stayed the rest of that day and night and wasn't seen by anyone till dawn broke the next day over the Liffey plain.

For fourteen years after that, Finn searched the country, exploring the remotest corners of the land in search of his beloved Sadb. All that time his face was sad, and he was never seen to smile. Except in the heat of battle or the excitement of a chase, his spirits never lifted. When he went hunting he left his main pack of dogs behind and took with him only Bran and Sceolan and three other hounds that he could trust. He wanted to be sure that Sadb would be left unharmed, if by good chance they ever found her.

Fourteen years after Sadb had been taken away, Finn and the Fianna were hunting on the side of Ben Bulben in Sligo when they heard the loud baying of the hounds ahead of them in a narrow pass. They rushed to the place to see what the clamor was about and found Finn's five hounds forming a circle round a naked youth whose long hair reached almost to his feet.

Finn's hounds were fighting furiously to hold back the rest of the pack as they tried to seize the boy. The youth stood calmly at the center of the circle, unconcerned by the turbulent dogfight that surged around his feet. He stared curiously at the men of the Fianna as they hurried to rescue him. As soon as the other dogs had been called off, Bran and Sceolan turned to the wild boy and whined and yelped at him, licking his face and limbs and jumping up on him as if he, and not Finn, were their master. Finn and his companions went up to the handsome youth and stroked his head gently and hugged him to show him he would not be harmed. They brought him with them to their hunting bothy and gave him food and drink.

When they returned to Almu, the youth came with them and there they gave him clothes and cut his hair, and gradually he began to be easy in their company and forgot his sudden, wild ways. Finn, staring intently at the boy, saw in his features a shadow of the lovely face of Sadb. He judged him to be about fourteen years of age, the number of years since Sadb had been spirited away, and he felt sure that the woodland boy was their child. Finn loved the youth and kept him at his side all day long. He talked to him and told him stories, and the boy learned to speak. Like their master, Bran and Sceolan loved their new companion and spent all their time playing around him, waiting to be petted. When the boy had learned to speak, he told Finn this story.

"It was a deer, a gentle doe, who protected me and sheltered me when I was a child. She cared for me night and day, and I loved her like a mother. We lived in a wild, lonely place, a mountain park, surrounded by high peaks and sheer cliffs. We stayed together all the time, ranging through valleys, over rocky slopes, drinking from the streams, hiding in the dark woods. We roamed through every corner of the region till we knew each hill and glen, but though we were free to wander where we liked in our mountain home, we were prisoners there. We couldn't escape because of the mountains and cliffs that circled it. During the summer we fed on berries and fruit, for there were plenty of them in the woods and hedges, and in the winter, provisions were left for me in a sheltered cave.

"A dark-haired man visited us from time to time. He would talk to the doe. Sometimes he spoke gently to her, sometimes he shouted at her in a loud, threatening voice, but no matter how he spoke to her, she shrank away from him with terrified eyes, every limb quivering with fear. The man could not get near her and he always left in a great rage.

"One day this man, the Dark Druid, arrived when we were beside a high cliff. He came close to the doe and spoke to her. At first he spoke tenderly to her, coaxing her to come away with him. Then he harangued her, threatening her in a loud, harsh voice. He kept this treatment up for a long time, but the doe still shrank away out of his reach, trembling and shaking.

Suddenly the Dark Druid moved close to the doe, cornering her in a narrow place, and took a hazel

wand and struck her with it. He cast a spell on her, and she was powerless
then to do anything except follow him. As the druid led her away, she kept
looking back at me, bleating and calling out with heartbroken cries. I was
sobbing, too, and I made desperate attempts to follow her but try as I might,
I could not move a limb for I, too, had been put under a spell. I was frightened and lonely and I shouted out again and again, but I could
do nothing but listen to the deer's cries grow fainter and more
desperate as she was taken away. In the end I was so over-
come with sadness that I fainted and fell to the ground.

"When I woke up, the hilly region where the doe
and I had lived so happily had gone, and I found
myself in a place I had never seen before. I
searched for days for the high mountains
and familiar cliffs, but I couldn't find them
anywhere. I wandered alone exploring the
new terrain for a few more days until I
heard the baying of the hounds as they
picked up my scent in the mountain pass.
Bran and Sceolan protected me till you,
Finn, and the men of the Fianna arrived
and brought me here to Almu."

When Finn heard this story he was happy,
for he knew for certain that the youth was
his child and the child of his beloved Sadb,
and he called the boy Oisin, which means
"Little Deer."

OISIN IN THE LAND OF YOUTH

UNDREDS OF YEARS AFTER FINN MAC CUMHAILL AND HIS companions had died, Saint Patrick came to Ireland and brought with him the Christian religion. As he traveled around the country preaching the gospel, he heard many stories about the adventures of Finn and the Fianna, and he became interested in these old heroes. Their story seemed to be written into the very landscape of Ireland; hills and woods resounded with their legends, rivers and valleys bore their names, dolmens marked their graves.

One day a feeble, blind old man was brought to Patrick. Patrick preached the new doctrines to him, but the old warrior defiantly sang the praises of the Fianna, their code of honor and their way of life. He said he was Oisin, the son of Finn himself.

Patrick doubted the old man's word, since Finn and his followers had been dead longer than the span of any human life. So to convince the saint that his claim was true, Oisin, the last of the Fianna, told this story:

The Battle of Gowra was the last battle that Finn and the Fianna ever fought. When it was over, only a handful of survivors were left, among them Finn and his son, Oisin. This little band escaped from the battlefield and made their way south to Lough Lene in Kerry, a favorite haunt of theirs in happier times.

One May morning, when the early mists were beginning to lift over the fresh, green woods around Lough Lene, Finn and his followers set out to hunt. The beauty of the countryside and the prospect of the chase revived their spirits a little as they followed the hounds through the woods. Suddenly a young, hornless deer broke cover and bounded through the forest with the dogs in full cry at its heels. The Fianna followed them, rejuvenated by the familiar excitement of the chase.

As they headed toward the coast, they were stopped in their tracks by the sight of a lovely young woman galloping toward them on a nimble white horse. She was as beautiful as a vision. Her eyes were as clear and blue as the May sky, and they sparkled like the dew on the bluebells at her feet. Around the horse's head and neck hung a golden bridle, and the shoes on its hooves were made of gold. In all their lives the Fianna had never seen a finer animal.

The woman approached. "I've traveled a great distance to find you," she said.

"Who are you and where have you come from?" Finn asked, moonstruck.

"I am called Niamh of the Golden Hair, and my father is the king of Tir na n-Og, the Land of Youth." the girl replied.

"Has tragedy brought you here?"

"No," she answered. "I came because I love your son."

Finn started in surprise. "You love one of my sons?"

"Oisin is the one," replied Niamh. "Reports of his handsome looks and sweet nature reached even as far as the Land of Youth, so I decided to come and find him."

Oisin had been silent all this time. But now he recovered himself. "You are the most beautiful woman in the world," he said, "and I would choose you above all others. I will gladly marry you!"

"Come away with me, Oisin!" Niamh whispered. "Come back with me to the Land of Youth. You will never fall ill or grow old there; you will never die. Trees grow tall there, and all year round the branches bow low with fruit. The land flows with honey and wine, as much as you could ever want. In Tir na n-Og you will sit at feasts and games, and there will be plenty of music for you, plenty of wine. You will have more gold than you could imagine, and a hundred swords, a hundred silk tunics, a hundred swift bay horses, a hundred keen hunting dogs. The king of the Ever Young will place a crown on your head, a crown that he has never given to anyone else, and it will protect you from every danger. As well as all of this, you will get beauty, strength, and power. And me for your wife."

"Oh, Niamh, I could never refuse you anything you ask." cried Oisin, and he jumped up on the horse behind her.

"Go slowly, Oisin, until we reach the shore!" Niamh cautioned.

When Finn saw his son being borne away from him toward the sea, he let out three loud, sorrowful shouts.

Oisin turned the horse back and dismounted. He embraced his father and said good-bye to all his friends. With tears streaming down his face he took a last look at them as they stood on the shore. He saw the defeat and sadness on his father's face and the sorrow of his friends. He remembered the happy times he had spent with them in the excitement of the chase and the heat of battle. But grief-stricken as he was, he could not stay, and he mounted the horse again and shook the reins. At that, the white horse tossed its mane, gave three shrill neighs, and leapt forward into the sea. The waves opened before Niamh and Oisin and closed behind them as they passed.

As they traveled through the waves, wonderful sights appeared on every side. They passed cities, courts, and castles, whitewashed bawns and forts, painted summerhouses fragrant with flowers, and stately palaces. A young fawn rushed past, a white dog with scarlet ears racing after it. A beautiful young woman on a bay horse galloped by on the crests of the waves, carrying a golden apple in her right hand; behind her rode a young noble-man, handsome and richly dressed with a gold-bladed sword in his hand.

Ahead of them, away in the distance, a shining palace came into view standing serenely on a hillside. Its delicate facade shone in the sun.

"What a handsome palace that is!" Oisin exclaimed. "Who lives there and what is the name of the country he rules?"

"This is the Land of Virtue, and that is the palace of Fomor, a ferocious giant," Niamh replied. "The daughter of the king of the Land of Life is the queen. She was abducted from her own court by Fomor, and he keeps her prisoner here. She has put a spell on him that he may not marry her until a champion has challenged him to single combat. But a prisoner she remains, for no one wants to fight the giant."

"Niamh, even though your voice is music to my ears, the story you have told me is sad," Oisin said. "I'll go to the fortress and try to over-come the giant and set the queen free."

They turned the horse toward the white palace, and when they arrived there they were welcomed by a woman almost as beautiful as Niamh herself. She seated them on golden chairs and, with tears spilling down her cheeks, she told them how much she longed to be free of Fomor.

"Dry your eyes," Oisin told her. "I'll challenge the giant. I'm not afraid of him! Either I'll kill him or I'll fight till he kills me."

At that moment, Fomor came into the castle, and when he saw Oisin, with a loud, angry roar he challenged him to a fight.

For three days and three nights they grappled. Powerful and fierce as Fomor was, Oisin overpowered him in the end and cut off his head. The two women gave three triumphant cheers when they saw the giant felled. Then they realized that Oisin was badly injured and exhausted. They took him gently between them and helped him back to the palace, where the queen put ointments and herbs on his wounds, and in a short time Oisin had recovered his health and spirits.

In the morning Niamh told Oisin that they must continue on their journey to Tir na n-Og. The sky darkened, the wind rose, and the boiling sea was lit by angry flashes. Niamh and Oisin rode steadily through the tempest, looking up at the pillars of cloud that glowed red, as lightning split the sky. As suddenly as it had begun, the storm abated, the fierce wind dropped, the waves calmed, and the sun shone brightly overhead.

There, amid the smooth, rich plains, a majestic castle glinted like a prism. Surrounding the castle were airy halls and summerhouses. As Niamh and Oisin approached the fortress, a troop of a hundred champions came out to meet them, their swords and shields shining in the sun.

Oisin was overwhelmed by the beauty of everything he saw. "Have we arrived at the Land of Youth?" he said at last.

"Indeed we have! This is Tir na n-Og," Niamh replied. "I told you the truth when I said how beautiful it was. And everything else I promised you, you will receive as well."

As Niamh spoke, a hundred beautiful young women came to meet them, dressed in silk and heavy brocade, and they welcomed the couple to Tir na n-Og. A huge, glittering crowd then approached and Oisin saw the king dressed in saffron silk, with a gold crown on his head, and beside him the queen, young and beautiful and attended by fifty girls who sang together as they crossed the green. When Niamh and Oisin met the royal party, the king took Oisin by the hand and welcomed him to his kingdom. Oisin thanked the king and queen, and a wedding feast was prepared for himself and Niamh. The festivities lasted for ten days and ten nights.

All that Niamh had promised came about, and Oisin lived happily in the Land of Youth with Niamh. Three children were born to them, and Niamh named one boy Finn in memory of Oisin's father and the other Oscar. Oisin gave his daughter a name that suited her loving nature and her lovely face; he named her Plur na mBan, the Flower of Women.

Three hundred years went by, though to Oisin they seemed as short as three. Then he began to get homesick for Ireland and lonely without the companionship of his friends, so he asked Niamh and her father to allow him to return home. The king consented, but Niamh begged him not to go.

Oisin tried to comfort his wife. "Don't be distressed, Niamh!" he said. "Our white horse knows the way. He'll bring me back safely."

So Niamh consented, but she gave Oisin a most solemn warning. "Listen to me, Oisin," she implored. "Do not dismount from the horse or you will never be able to return to this happy country. I say it again: If your foot as much as touches the ground while you are in Ireland, you will be lost forever to the Land of Youth!"

Then Niamh began to sob and wail. "Oisin, for the third time I warn you: Do not set foot on the soil of Ireland or you can never come back to me again. You should not go back, anyway! Everything is changed there. You will not see Finn or the Fianna. You will find only a crowd of monks and holy men."

Oisin consoled his wife as best he could, but Niamh pulled and clutched at her hair. His children were standing by, and as Oisin said farewell to them, his heart was heavy. As he stood by the white horse Niamh came up to him and kissed him. "Oh, Oisin," she sobbed, "here is a last kiss for you! You will never come back to me or the Land of Youth."

With a heavy heart Oisin mounted his horse and set out for Ireland. The horse took him away from Tir na n-Og as swiftly as it had brought Niamh and him there three hundred years before.

By the time Oisin arrived in Ireland, he was in high spirits, as strong and powerful a champion as he had ever been, and he set out at once to find the Fianna. He traveled over the familiar terrain where he had traveled so often with his companions, but saw no trace of any one of them. He went from one of Finn's haunts to another, but they were all deserted. He set out for the plains of Leinster and Almu, the place that he loved best. But when he arrived, there was no trace of the shining white fort. There was only a bare, windswept hill overgrown with ragwort, chickweed, and nettles. Oisin was heartbroken at the sight of the desolate place, and a tide of weariness washed over him as he realized that Finn and his companions were dead. With a heavy heart he left the Hill of Allen and headed eastward.

As he passed through Wicklow, through Glenasmole, the Valley of the Thrushes, he saw three hundred or more people crowding the glen. As Oisin approached, they stared at him curiously, astonished at his appearance and his great size. Then one of them shouted urgently, "Come over here and help us! You are much stronger than we are!" Oisin brought his horse closer to the crowd and saw that they were trying to lift up a vast marble flagstone. The stone was so great that the men underneath could not support it and were being crushed by the weight. Some were down already. Again the leader shouted desperately to Oisin, "Come quickly and help us lift the slab or all these men will be crushed to death!" Oisin looked down in disbelief at the crowd of men beneath him who were so puny and weak that they were unable to lift the flagstone. He leaned out of the saddle and, taking the marble slab in his hands, he raised it with all his strength and flung it away and the men underneath it were freed. But the slab was so heavy and the exertion so great that the golden girth round the horse's belly snapped, and Oisin was pulled sideways out of the saddle. He had to jump to the ground to save himself from falling, and the instant its rider's feet touched the ground, the horse bolted and galloped like the wind out of sight. Oisin stood upright for a moment, towering over the gathering. Then as the horrified crowd watched, the tall, young warrior, who had been stronger than all of them together, sank slowly to the ground. His powerful body withered and shrank, the skin on his handsome face wrinkled and sagged, and the sight left his clouded eyes. Hopeless and helpless, he lay at their feet, a bewildered, blind old man. But he lived to tell the tale, as did other tale-tellers after him. Patrick's scribes wrote these stories down and that is why Oisin and Finn, the Red Branch Heroes and the Tuatha De Danaan live on through their legends to this day.

PRONUNCIATION GUIDE

PRONUNCIATION OF IRISH NAMES AND WORDS

The following gives an approximate guide to the pronunciation of the Irish names and words that occur in the stories. Because there are both vowel and consonant sounds in the Irish language that do not exist in English, it is difficult to render the original sounds faithfully. What follows, therefore, is a simplified version of those sounds. The syllable that is stressed is in italics, and some words, whose pronunciation seems obvious, are included to indicate where the accent lies. Sometimes there is more than one way to pronounce the same word and I have given these alternatives where relevant.

To make reading aloud easier, I have given separate pronunciation notes for each story. They are in order of appearance.

Sidhe   shee

MOYTURA
Moytura   moy-*toor*-a
Tuatha De Danaan   *too*-ha day *dan*-an
Fomorians   fo-*more*-ee-ans
Nuada   *noo*-a-ha
Balor   *bah*-lor
Eithlinn   *eth*-leen
Cian   *kee*-an
Birog   *birr*-ogue
Lugh   loo
Camall   *cam*-all
Ceithlinn   *keth*-leen
Morrigu (the)   *morr*-ig-oo

THE CHILDREN OF LIR
Fionnuala   finn-*noo*-la
Aed   ay (rhymes with day)
Fiacra   *fee*-ak-ra
Aoife   *eef*-eh
Bodb Dearg   bov *jar*-ag

Tuatha De Danaan   *too*-ha day *dan*-an
Derravaragh   der-ra-*va*-an
Carraignarone   carrig-na-*rone*
Mochaomhog   mo-*keev*-og
Lairgren   *lye*-er-gren

THE BIRTH OF CUCHULAINN
Cuchulainn   koo-*hull*-in / koo-*kull*-in
Conor Mac Nessa   *kon*-or mac *ness*-a
Emain Macha   *ev*-in *mach*-a / *ow*-in *mach*-a
  (ow rhymes with how)
Dechtire   *deck*-tir-a
Slieve Fuad   sleeve *foo*-ad
Bricriu   *brick*-roo
Lugh   loo
Finnchoem   *fin*-koo-em
Sencha   *shen*-ha
Morann   *mor*-an
Blai   *bla*-ee
Fergus   *fer*-gus
Amergin   *ah*-mer-gin / *ah*-ver-gin (hard g)
Dun Breth   doon breth

Sualdam Mac Roich   *soo*-al-dav mack *roy*
Setanta   shay-*tant*-a
Culann   *kull*-in
Cathbad   *kath*-vad / *kaff*-a

BRICRIU'S FEAST
Bricriu   *brick*-roo
Dun Rudraige   doon *ro*-ry
Emain Macha   *ev*-in *mach*-a / *ow*-in *mach*-a
   (ow rhymes with how)
Fergus   *fer*-gus
Laoghaire   *lair*-eh
Conall Cearnach   *kon*-all *kar*-nah
Cuchulainn   koo-*hull*-in / koo-*kull*-in
Sencha   *shen*-ha
Fidelma   fid-*dell*-ma
Lendabar   *len*-da-var
Emer   *ay*-ver / *ay*-mer
   (*ay* rhymes with day)
Cu Roi   koo *ree*

DEIRDRE OF THE SORROWS
Deirdre   *der*-dru
   (the u is barely sounded)
Felimid   *fell*-im-eed
Cathbad   *kath*-vad / *kaff*-a
Conor Mac Nessa   *kon*-or mac *ness*-a
Levercham   *lev*-er-ham
Naoise   *neesh*-eh
Usnach   *oosh*-na
Ardan   *aw*-ar-dawn
Ainnle   *awn*-leh
geis   gesh
Fergus   *fer*-gus
Dubhtach   *duv*-tah / *duff*-ach
Cormac   *kor*-moc
Emain Macha   *ev*-in *mach*-a / *ow*-in *mach*-a
   (ow rhymes with how)

Borrach   *bor*-ack
Fiacha   *fee*-ach-a
Eogan   *oh*-en (Owen)

THE SALMON OF KNOWLEDGE
Almu   *al*-moo
Tadg   *ta*-ig
Muirne   *mur*-na
Cumhaill   kool
Bascna   *bask*-na
Fianna   *fee*-a-na
Morna   *mor*-na
Cnuca   k-*nuck*-a
Demne   *dem*-na
Goll   gawl
Finn Mac Cumhaill   fin ma *kool*
Crimhall   *kriv*-al
Finnegas   fin-*ay*-gas (ay rhymes with day)

THE ENCHANTED DEER
Finn Mac Cumhaill   fin ma *kool*
Almu   *al*-moo
Sceolan   *skow*-lan
Sadb   sive (rhymes with dive)
Tuatha De Danaan   *too*-ha day *dan*-an
Fianna   *fee*-a-na
Lochlann   *loch*-lan
Oisin   ush-*een*

OISIN IN THE LAND OF YOUTH
Oisin   ush-*een*
Finn Mac Cumhaill   fin ma *kool*
Gowra   *gow*-ra (gow rhymes with how)
Niamh   *nee*-uv
Tir na n-Og   teer na nogue
Fomor   *foe*-more
Plur na mBan   *ploor* na *mawn*

SOURCE NOTES

I have listed below the main source or sources that I used for each story. I have added a further list of books which I found particularly helpful. Some of these are academic studies, and some are retellings. Incidents and details from a few of them have been incorporated here and there in my text.

THE MYTHOLOGICAL CYCLE

Moytura

Gray, Elizabeth A., *Cathe maig Tuired, The Second Battle of Mag Tuired*, Irish Texts Society, Dublin, 1982

Gregory, Augusta, *Gods and Fighting Men*, London, 1904

The Children of Lir

O'Curry, Eugene, "The Three Most Sorrowful Tales of Erinn," from *Atlantis IV*, Dublin, 1858

THE ULSTER CYCLE

The Birth of Cuchulainn

Hull, Eleanor (ed.), *The Cúchullin Saga in Irish Literature*, London, 1898

Bricriu's Feast

Cross, Tom Peete and Slover, Clark H., *Ancient Irish Tales*, London, 1937

Deirdre of the Sorrows

O'Flanagan, Theophilus, "Deirdri," *Transactions of the Gaelic Society of Dublin*, 1808

THE FINN CYCLE

Finn and the Salmon of Knowledge

Hennessy, W.M., *Revenue Celtique* II, Paris, 1873–5

Kennedy, Patrick, *Legendary Fictions of the Irish Celts*, London 1891

O'Donovan, John, "The Boyish Exploits of Finn Mac Cumhill" from *Transactions of the Ossianic Society* IV, Dublin, 1859

O'Grady, Standish Hayes, *Silva Gadelica*, Dublin, 1892

Mac Neill, Eoin, *Duanaire Finn* I, Irish Texts Society, London, 1908

The Enchanted Deer

Kennedy, Patrick, *Legendary Fictions of the Irish Celts*, London, 1891

Oisin in the Land of Youth

O'Looney, B., *Transactions of the Ossianic Society* IV, Dublin, 1859

Joyce, P.W., *Old Celtic Romances*, London, 1914

Cross, Tom Peete and Slover, Clark H., *Ancient Irish Tales*, London, 1937

Campbell, J.J., *Legends of Ireland*, London, 1955

Coghlan, Ronan, *Pocket Dictionary of Irish Myth and Legend*, Belfast, 1985

Curtain, Jeremiah, *Hero Tales of Ireland*, Dublin, 1894

Dillon, Myles *The Cycle of the Kings*, London, 1947

—*Early Irish Literature*, Chicago, 1948

—*Irish Sagas*, Dublin, 1954

Ellis, P. Berresford, *A Dictionary of Irish Mythology*, London, 1987

Flower, Robin, *The Irish Tradition*, Oxford, 1947

Green, Miranda J., *A Dictionary of Celtic Myth and Legend*, London, 1992

Gregory, Augustus, *The Blessed Trinity of Ireland*, London, 1985

Hull, Eleanor, *Cuchulain—the Hound of Ulster*, London, 1909

Hyde, Douglas, *The Three Sorrows of Storytelling*, London, 1895

Jackson, Kenneth Hurlstone, *A Celtic Miscellany*, London, 1951

Kavanagh, Peter, *Irish Mythology*, New York, 1959

Kinsella, Thomas, *The Tain*, Oxford, 1970

Kinsella, Thomas (ed.), *The New Oxford Book of Irish Verse*, Oxford, 1986

Mac Cana, Proinsias, *Celtic Mythology*, London, 1970

Mac Neill, Eoin, *Duanaire Finn* I, London, 1908

Meyer, Kuno, *Death Tales of the Ulster Heroes*, Dublin, 1913

—and Nutt, Alfred, *The Voyage of Bran, Son of Febal*, London, 1895

Montague, John (ed.), *The Faber Book of Irish Verse*, London, 1974

Murphy, Gerard, *Duanaire Finn* II, London, 1933

Nutt, Alfred, *Ossian and Ossianic Literature*, London, 1899

—*Cúchulainn: The Irish Achilles*, London, 1900

O'Connor, Frank, *Kings, Lords and Commons: An Anthology from the Irish*, New York, 1959

—*The Little Monasteries*, Dublin, 1963

O'Faolain, Eileen, *Irish Sagas and Folk Tales*, London, 1954

O'Grady, Standish Hayes, *Silva Gadelica*, 2 vols, Dublin, 1893

O'Grady, Standish James, *Fionn and His Companions*, Dublin, 1892

—*The Coming of Cuchulain*, London, 1894

—*The Triumph and Passing of Cuchulain*, London, 1920

O'Hogain, Daithi, *Myth, Legend and Romance*, London, 1990

O'Rahilly, Cecile, *Táin Bó Cuailgne* (from the Book of Leinster), Dublin, 1967

—*Táin Bó Cuailgne* (from the Book of the Dun Cow), Dublin, 1978

O'Rahilly, Thomas F., *Early Irish History and Mythology*, Dublin 1946

Rees, Alwyn and Brinley, *Celtic Heritage*, London, 1961

Rolleston, T.W., *Myths and Legends of the Celtic Race*, London, 1912

—*The High Deeds of Fionn*, London, 1910

Smyth, Daragh, *A Guide to Irish Mythology*, Dublin, 1988

Sjoestedt, M.L., *Gods and Heroes of the Celts*, Paris, 1949

Stephens, James, *Irish Fairy Tales*, London, 1924

THIS BOOK WAS DESIGNED BY KRISTINA ALBERTSON.

THE ART FOR THE BOTH THE JACKET AND THE

INTERIOR WAS CREATED BY P.J. LYNCH, USING

WATERCOLORS AND GOUACHE ON ARCHES PAPER. THE

TEXT WAS SET IN 12-POINT ARIES, A TYPEFACE DESIGNED

BY ERIC GILL IN 1932. CALLIGRAPHY BY BERNARD

MAISNER. THE BOOK WAS PRINTED AND BOUND AT

TIEN WAH PRESS IN SINGAPORE. PRODUCTION WAS

SUPERVISED BY ANGELA BIOLA AND ALISON FORNER.